Buck and Libby grow bigger than Arlo.

Solve the maze to help **BUCK** and **Libby** find **Arlo**.

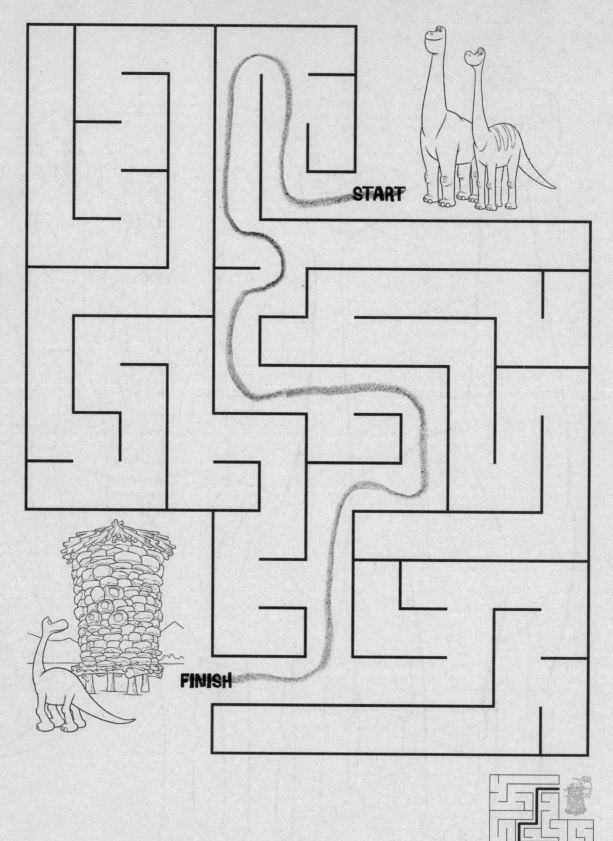

START

FINISH

Feeding the family's animals is **ArLo's** job.

Everyone has made a mark for doing something
big for the family. Except **ArLo**.

Place your hand on this page and
trace it to make your own mark.
Decorate it any way you like!

Replace each letter with the one that comes after it in the alphabet. Write the letters on the lines to complete the sentence.

K N U D R

Arlo is scared a lot of the time,
but **Poppa** _h_ _e_ _l_ _p_ _s_ him.

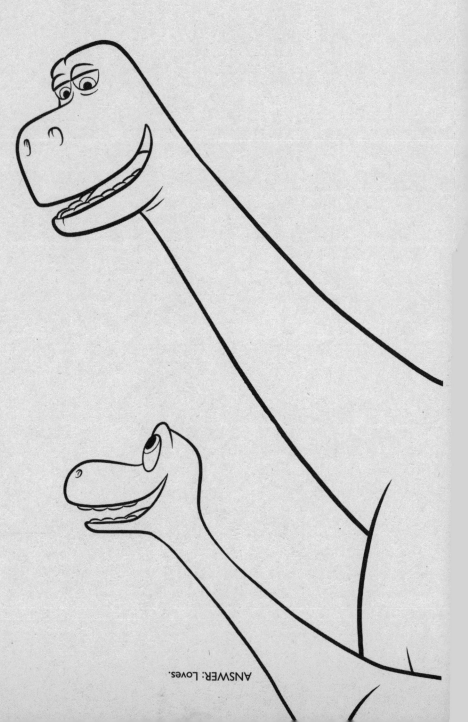

Poppa knows that **ArLo** will make his mark someday.

ArLo is even afraid of little fireflies!

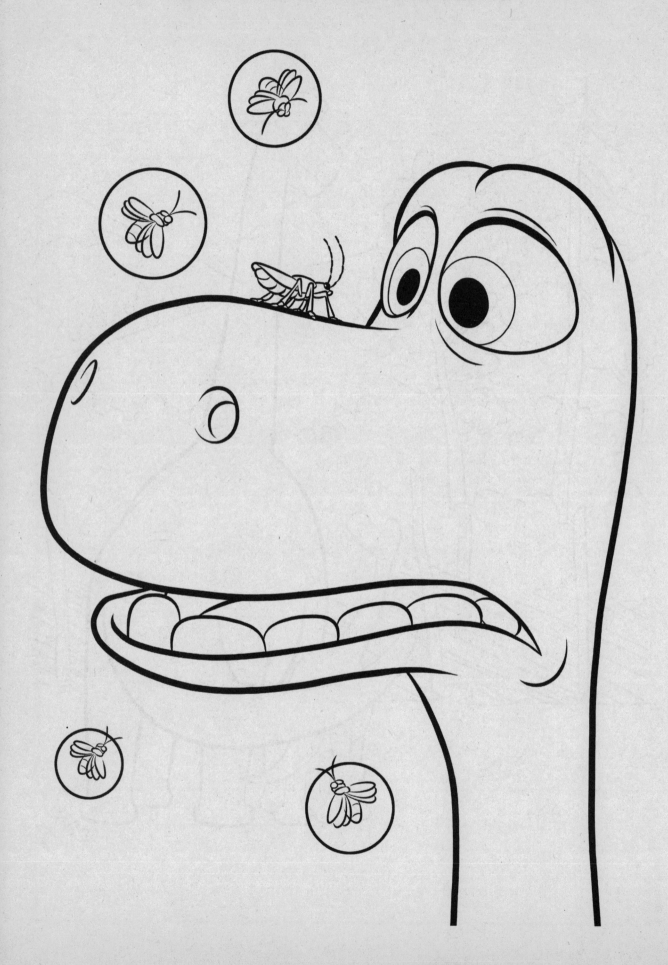

With **Poppa** gone, **Arlo** helps even more with the harvest.

Which two pictures are exactly the same?

This is one crazy critter!

Connect the dots to see what's going on!

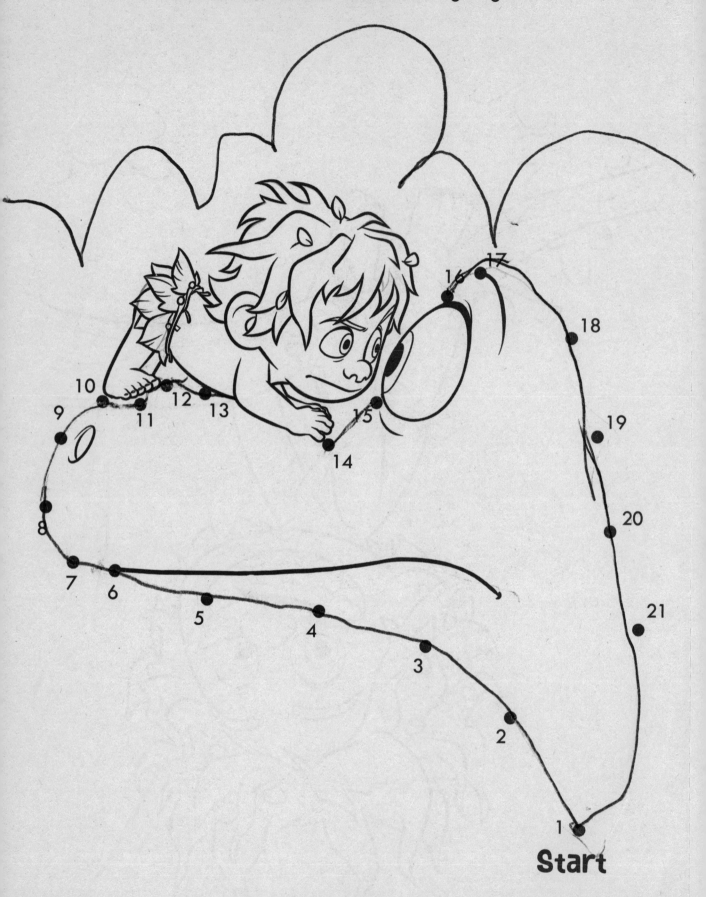

Start

Oh, no! The critter is on **ArLo's** nose!

Arlo falls into the river after a tussle with the scary critter!

Arlo and the critter fight over a piece of corn. With a friend, take turns drawing a line to connect two dots. If the line you draw completes a box, give yourself one point. When no more boxes can be made, the player with more points wins.

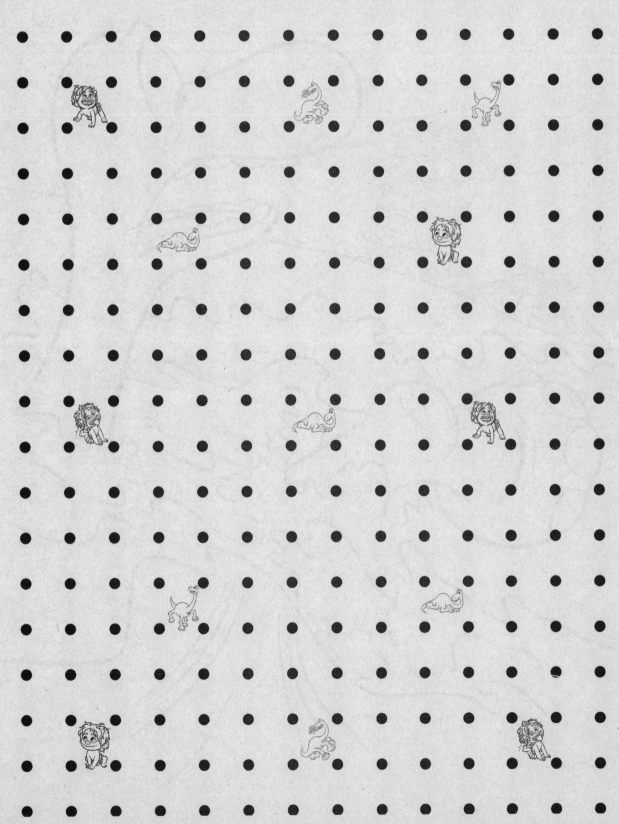

The river takes **ArLo** far away from home.

Arlo tries to get a bite to eat. Draw what you think it is.

ArLo is hungry. He tries to get berries.

ArLo slips and gets his foot trapped.

It is raining, but **ArLo's** shelter isn't very good.

Circle three differences between the two pictures.

ANSWER: Spot's pupils are not filled in, his eyebrows are black, and his top teeth are missing.

The critter goes on a wild ride!

The critter battles a bug. With a friend, take turns drawing a line to connect two dots. If the line you draw completes a box, give yourself one point. When no more boxes can be made, the player with more points wins.

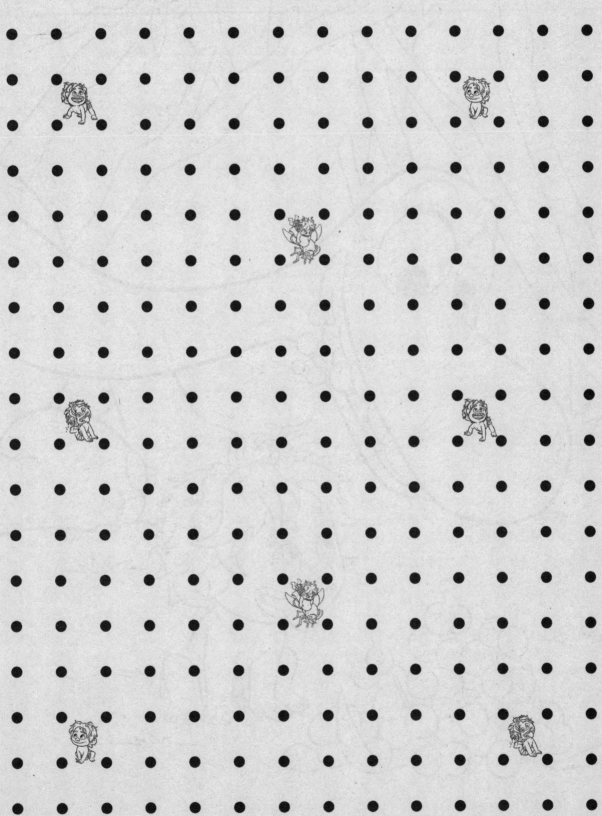

The critter brings **Arlo** berries. Yummy!

The critter plays hide-and-seek with **Arlo**.

How many words can you make from the letters in

APATOSAURUS?

POSSIBLE ANSWERS: Pat, pop, pot, rat, rust, sap, sat, soar, spot, star, tour, and us.

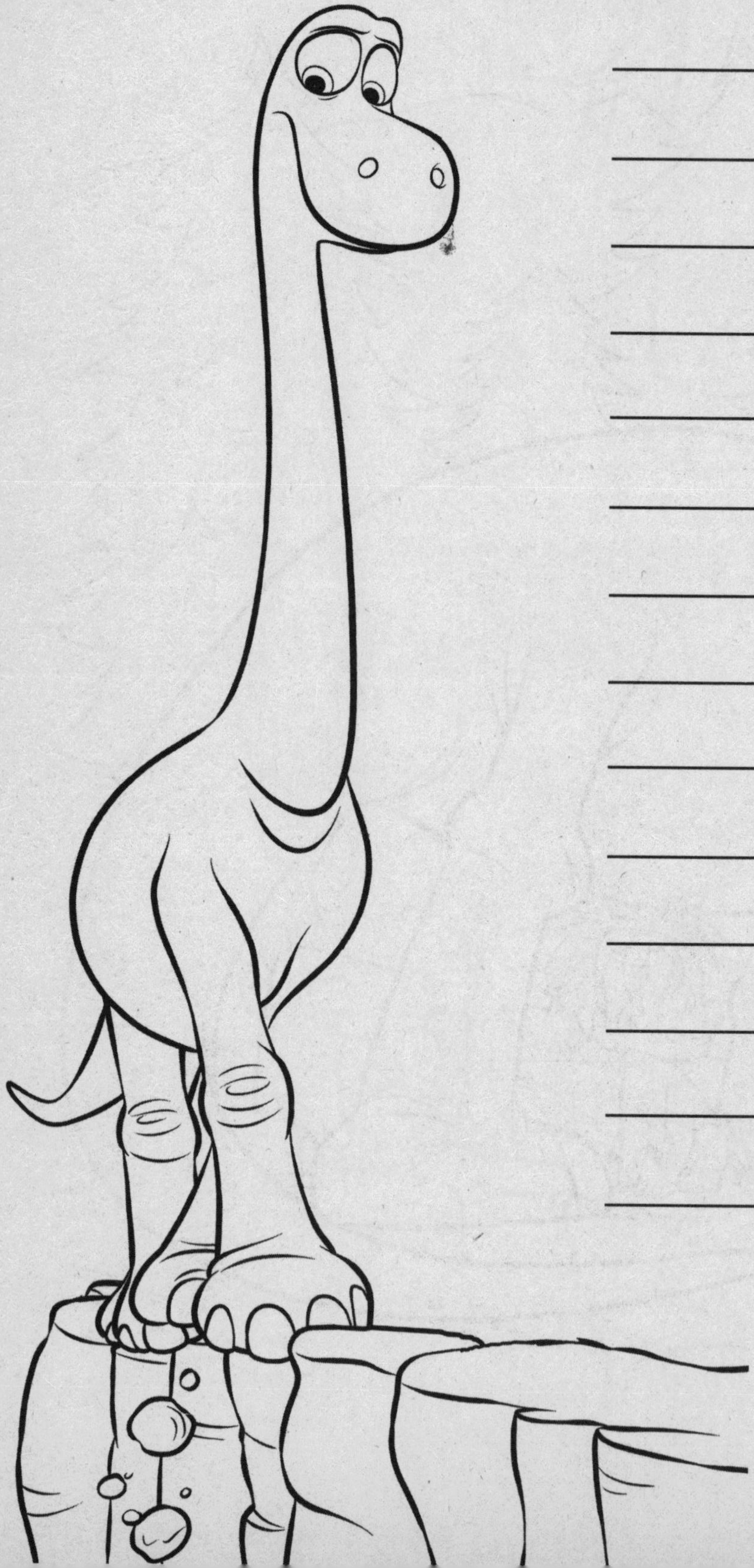

Spot has found something. Draw what you think it is.

The critter finds gophers! He teaches **ArLo** how to play with them.

How many gophers can you count on this page?

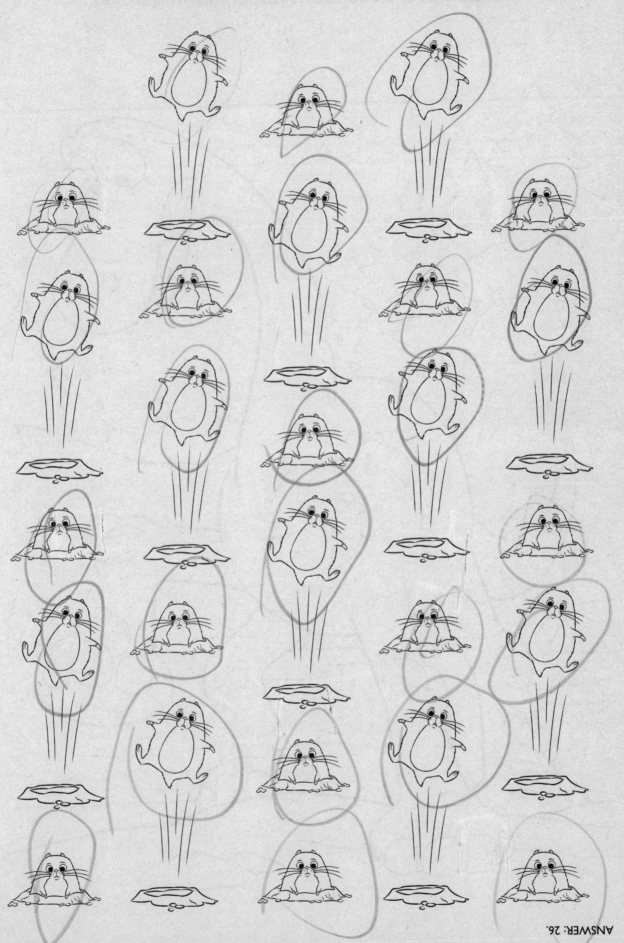

ANSWER: 26.

ArLo has a lot to learn about the wilderness.

Lots of animals like to hang out with **Forrest Woodbush.**

How many creatures can you count
on **Forrest Woodbush's** horns?

Arlo calls out several names, but the critter only responds to **Spot**!

Use the code to find out the names
Arlo and Forrest called.

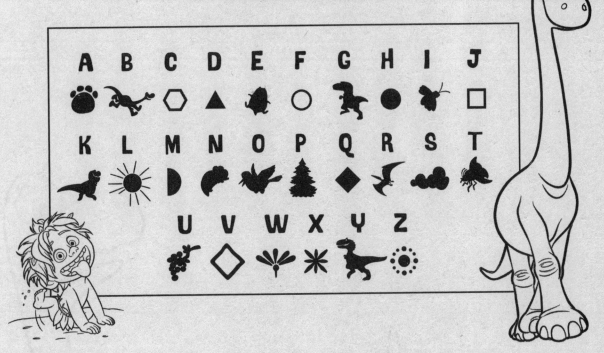

1. _ _ _ _ _ _

2. _ _ _ _ _ _

3. _ _ _ _ _ _

4. _ _ _ _ _

5. _ _ _ _ _ _

6. _ _ _ _ _

ANSWER: 1. Killer, 2. Stinky, 3. Beast, 4. Spike, 5. Grubby, and 6. Spot.

Something is frightening **ArLo**! Draw what you think it is.

Debbie tries to stop **Arlo** from taking **Spot**.
She wants to keep him.

ARLO shows **Spot** how to chase fireflies.
It reminds Arlo of his family.

How many fireflies can you count on this page?

Spot shows **Arlo** that he lost his family.

ArLo finds a way to show **Spot** what his family looks like.

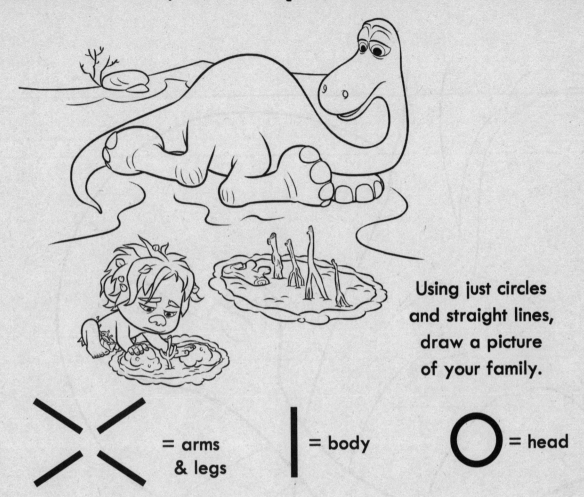

Using just circles and straight lines, draw a picture of your family.

✕ = arms & legs

❘ = body

⭕ = head

ArLo learns how to howl.

Can you find three differences in the bottom picture?

ANSWER: One stick figure is missing, one of the rocks in front of Spot is missing, and Arlo is missing a toenail.

Spot is becoming a friend!

ArLo sees something in the sky. Draw what you think it is.

Arlo thinks the Pterodactyl can help him find the way home.

Thunderclap is the leader of the Pterodactyls.

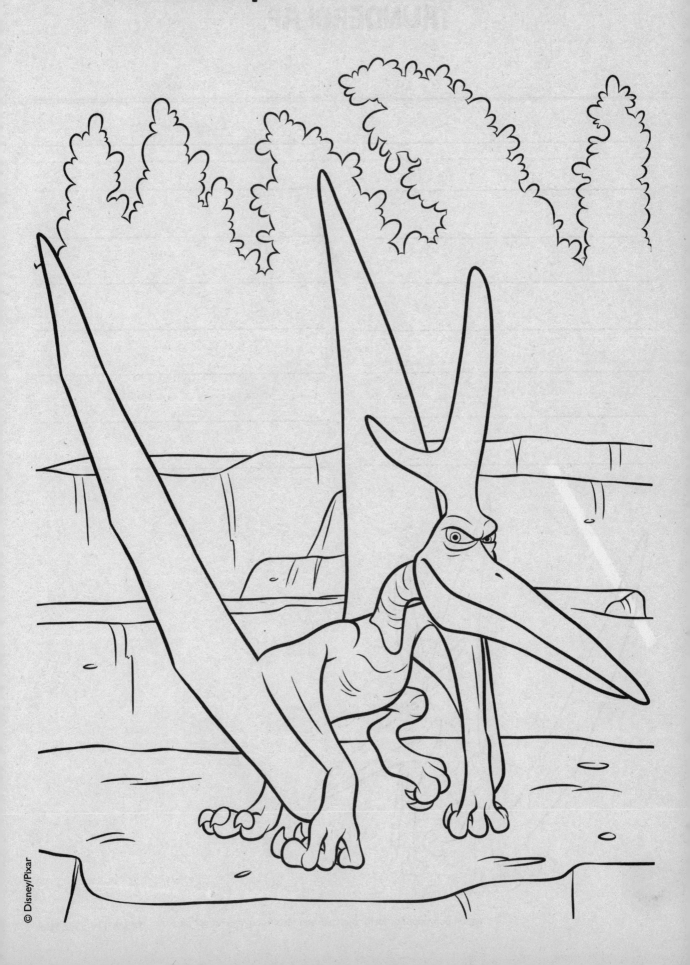

How many words can you make from the letters in
THUNDERCLAP.

_____   _____

_____   _____

_____   _____

_____   _____

_____   _____

_____   _____

_____   _____

_____   _____

Nash is Ramsey's brother.

Name some of your favorite things that begin with the letters in T. rex.

T _____

R _____

E _____

X _____

Nash makes some music.

Ramsey is Nash's sister.

Butch wants **Arlo's** help.

Match the T. rexes to their close-ups.

A   1

B   2

C   3

Butch is the oldest T. rex. Help him track his lost herd.

START

FINISH

Butch tells a story about a crocodile fight.

Butch battles a crocodile. With a friend, take turns drawing a line to connect two dots. If the line you draw completes a box, give yourself one point. When no more boxes can be made, the player with more points wins.

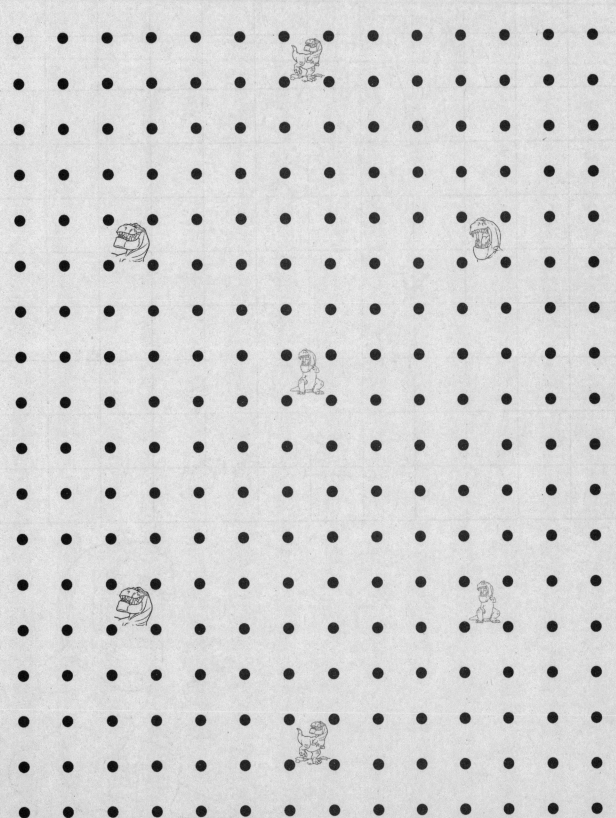

Finish this picture of **Butch**. Use the grid to help you.

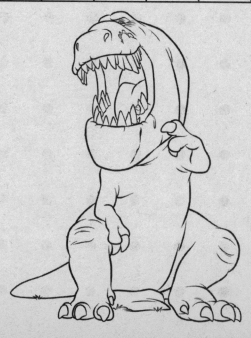

Arlo needs to call the Raptors out of hiding.
Spot helps him holler extra loudly.

The Raptors hear **Arlo** and come running.
Solve the maze to help **Arlo** escape.

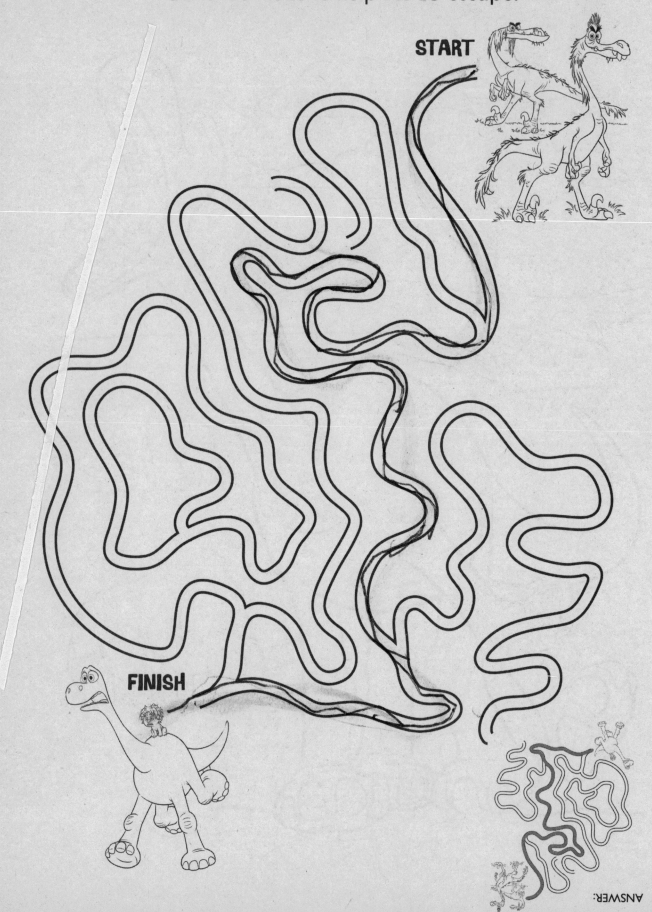

START

FINISH

The Raptors are mean.

Chase away the Raptors. With a friend, take turns
drawing a line to connect two dots. If the line you draw
completes a box, give yourself one point. When no more
boxes can be made, the player with more points wins.

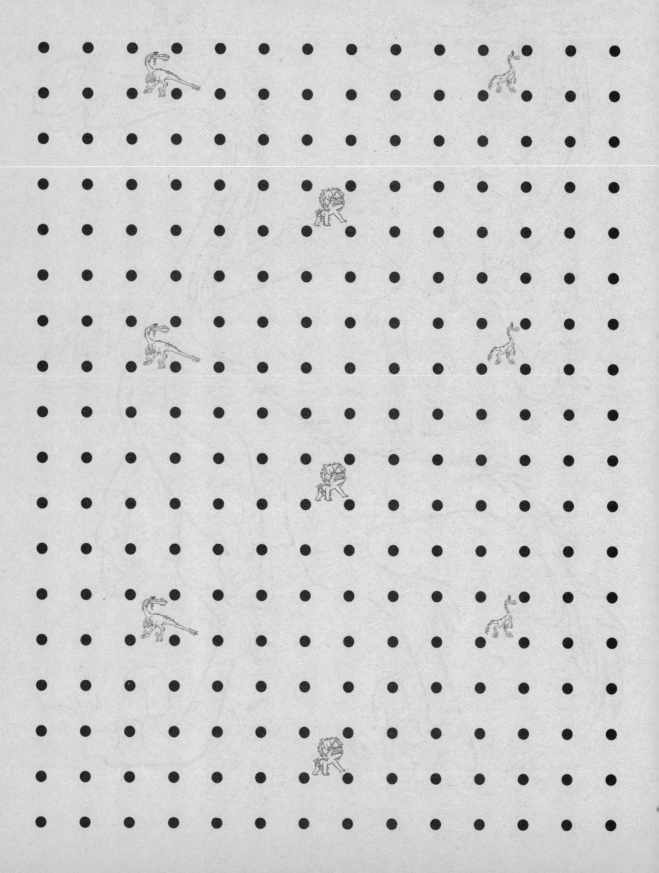

Which words describe **Spot**, and which words describe **Arlo?**

Look at each word and then write it in the correct column.

TALL · SMALL · BIG · HUMAN · HAIRY · GREEN

SPOT   ARLO

_____   _____

_____   _____

_____   _____

Make up a song about dinosaurs and write the words on the lines. Now sing it out loud!

_____

_____

_____

_____

_____

_____

_____

_____

_____

Can you count how many creatures are in the herd?

ANSWER: 27.

Butch tells a scary story. Make up your own scary story and write it on the lines.

_____

_____

_____

_____

_____

_____

_____

_____

Circle the three pictures of **Spot** that are exactly the same.

ANSWER: A, B, and D.

ArLo can see home!

Use the key to solve the code. Write the letters on the lines.

Arlo and Spot see the top of

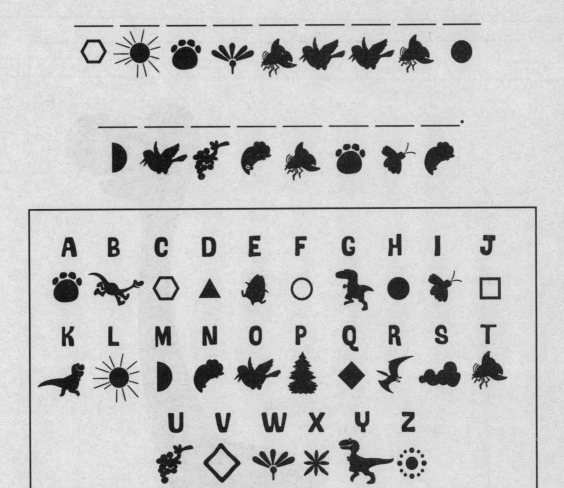

Unscramble the letters to reveal the name of this dinosaur.

SAOTUASURAP

_ _ _ _ _ _ _ _ _ _ _ _

Spot sees something. Draw what you think it is.

ArLo is afraid that Spot might want to leave him.

ArLo and **Spot** see something. Draw what you think it is.

The Pterodactyls have found them.

How many Pterodactyls can you count?

Draw any kind of wings you like on **Thunderclap**.

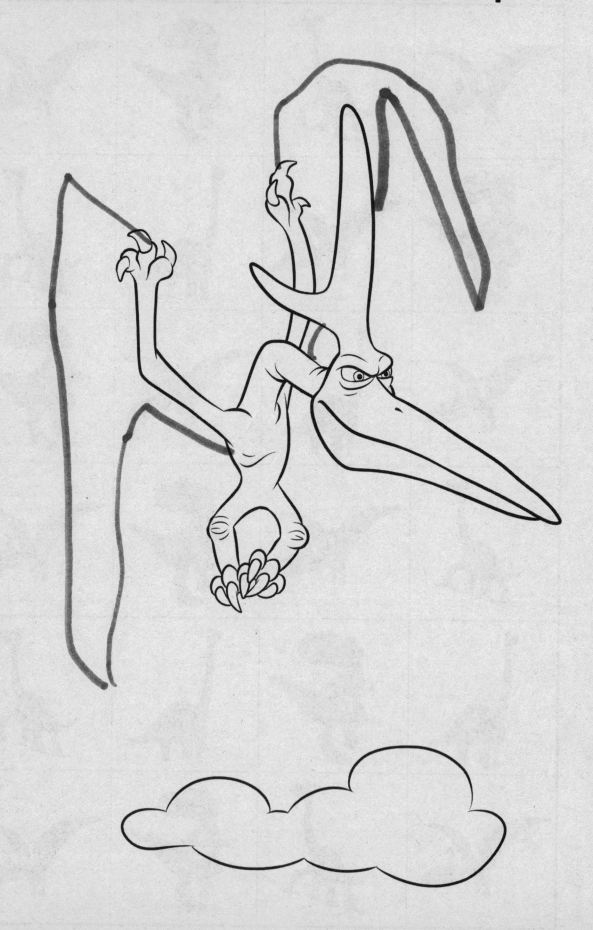

Thunderclap grabs Spot!

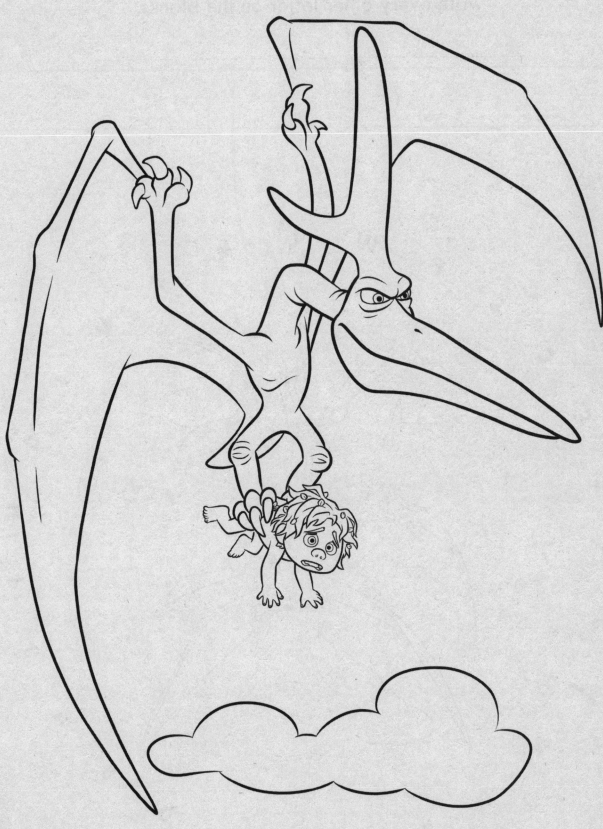

Pterodactyls aren't dinosaurs. What are they? Start at the arrow and, going clockwise around the circle, write every other letter on the blanks.

_ _ _ _ _ _   _ _ _ _ _ _ _ _

Circle the three differences between the top and bottom pictures.

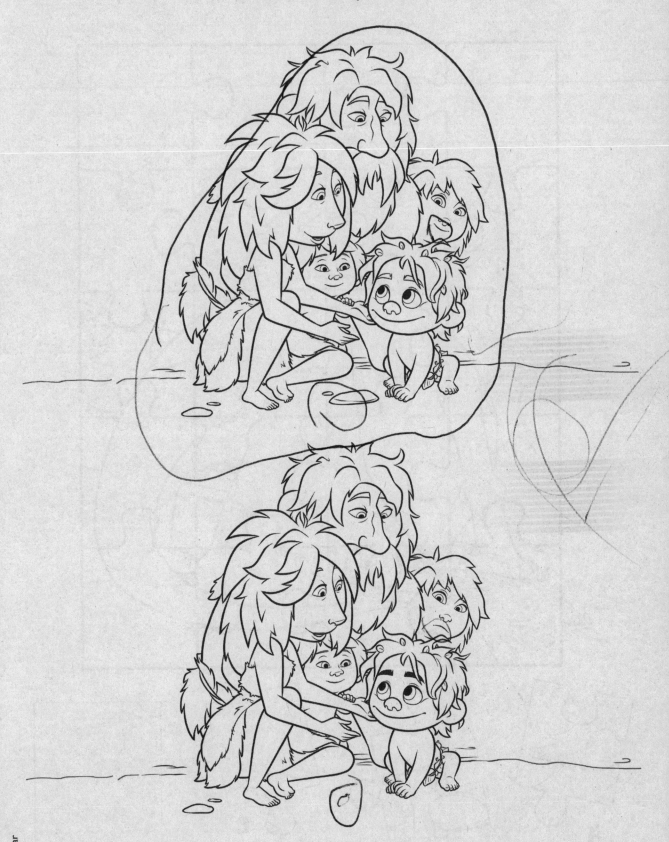

ANSWER: Spot's eyebrows are filled in, a rock is missing, and Spot's new brother is frowning.

Can you find where each puzzle piece belongs in the picture of **ArLo** and **Spot** below?

Draw yourself or a member of your family as a caveperson.

Match the members of Spot's new family to their close-ups.

A

B

C

Who in your family is most like a caveperson?

Who is most like a dinosaur?

Which one are you like?

Caveperson: _____

Why? _____
_____
_____
_____

Dinosaur: _____

Why? _____
_____
_____
_____

YOU! _____

Why? _____
_____
_____
_____

Arlo wishes his friend didn't have to go. With a friend, take turns drawing a line to connect two dots. If the line you draw completes a box, give yourself one point. When no more boxes can be made, the player with more points wins.

Play again! With a friend, take turns drawing a line to connect two dots. If the line you draw completes a box, give yourself one point. When no more boxes can be made, the player with more points wins.

Arlo and **Spot** will miss each other.

Draw yourself hugging someone special.

ArLo finds his way home.

How many times can you find and circle the words
ARLO and HOME in the puzzle?

P	T	E	H	O	M	E	O
Y	A	R	L	O	K	H	A
O	M	K	H	O	M	E	R
A	R	H	P	G	M	H	L
R	E	A	O	L	O	H	O
L	B	L	X	M	B	C	L
O	R	R	E	O	E	M	O
A	U	Z	P	E	M	O	H

ANSWER: Arlo: 4; home: 5.

Arlo is getting closer and closer to home.
Draw what he is thinking.

ArLo took care of the critter. He finally makes his mark.

There are lots of these animals on the farm.

Trace your foot on this page.
Then add some claws to your toes for fun!

Who's Hiding?

Match the numbered piece of the picture with the identical scrambled piece from the other picture. Write the correct number under each scrambled piece. For added fun, have an adult help you cut out the scrambled pieces. Then put them together in the correct order, just like a puzzle!

1 2 3 4 5 6 7 8

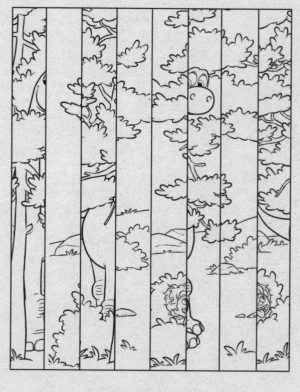

How many teeth does this T. rex have? Count them.

ANSWER: 26.

Use the key to decipher the code and reveal what the T. rex says to Spot.

_____ _____, _____!

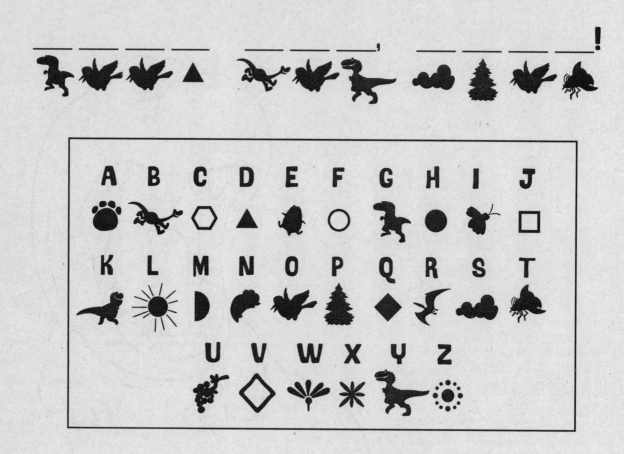

How many times can you find **TREX** in the puzzle below?

T	R	E	X	X	T	R	T
X	X	E	R	T	E	R	R
T	R	T	X	T	E	X	E
R	T	R	E	X	T	R	X
E	R	E	R	E	E	R	E
X	E	X	T	R	X	R	T
E	X	T	E	T	T	E	T
R	T	X	R	T	R	E	X

ANSWER: 12.

The T. rex family is on the move.

Draw a Raptor for **Butch** to scare off.

The Pterodactyls attack. With a friend, take turns drawing a line to connect two dots. If the line you draw completes a box, give yourself one point. When no more boxes can be made, the player with more points wins.

Play again! With a friend, take turns drawing a line to connect two dots. If the line you draw completes a box, give yourself one point. When no more boxes can be made, the player with more points wins.

Use the key to color the scene.

1 = Brown   **2** = Green   **3** = Gray   **4** = Sky-Blue

Place these words in the correct boxes.

APATOSAURUS · PTERODACTYL · RAPTORS
STYRACOSAURUS · TYRANNOSAURUS REX
TRICERATOPS

R (across, row 1)

R (down)

T (across, row 2)

R (down)

T (across, row 3)

A (across, row 4)

S (across, row 5)

Something is missing. Do you see what it is?
Can you add it?

Use the key to color the scene.

1 = Brown   2 = Tan   3 = Green   4 = Gray

Round up the creatures on the farm. With a friend, take turns drawing a line to connect two dots. If the line you draw completes a box, give yourself one point. When no more boxes can be made, the player with more points wins.

Help **Arlo** harvest the corn by solving the maze.

START

FINISH

ANSWER:

Use the key to color the image.

1 = Green **2 = Brown** **3 = Tan** **4 = Gray** **5 = Yellow**

Something is getting in **ArLo's** face.
Draw what you think it is.

Compare the top picture and the bottom picture.
Can you find three differences in the bottom picture?

Arlo is getting rained on.
Draw a new scene with Arlo in the sun!

Use the key to color the image.

1 = Green   2 = Brown   3 = Gray   4 = Sky-Blue

Start at the arrow and, going clockwise around the circle, write every other letter on the blanks.

___ ___ ___ ___ ___, ___ ___ ___ ___ ___ ___!

Put the words in the correct boxes to solve the puzzle.

TREE · RIVER · ROCK · BUSHES
MOUNTAIN · SKY

To find out what Arlo is thinking, cross out all
the Cs and write the remaining letters on the blanks.

RCCCAICNRCAINCCGOCACWACYC

—— —— —— —— , —— —— —— —— , —— —— —— —— —— .

ANSWER: Rain, rain, go away.

To reveal the message, start at the arrow and, going clockwise, around the triangle, write every other letter on the lines.

__ _____

___ _____ .

Draw a storm over **ArLo**.

Draw who you think is hiding from **Arlo**.

Connect the dots to reveal the scene.

START

© Disney/Pixar

To reveal the message, cross out all the Gs and
write the remaining letters in order on the lines.

GGBGEGGGSGGT   GGGFGRGIGGEGNDGGGSG

_____   _____

ANSWER: Best friends.

Can you find the three differences between the top and bottom pictures?

ANSWER: A rock is missing, a tree is missing, and Spot is missing a tooth.

To reveal the message, start at the arrow and, going clockwise around the circle, write the letters on the line.

Arlo and Spot get

_____.

Use only the letters in **ARLO** to complete this sentence.

SP_T ST___ES _T _N_ THE_ HUM_N.

© Disney/Pixar

ANSWER: Spot stares at another human.

Can you find three differences between the top and bottom pictures?

Spot is in trouble. Use the key to decode his message.

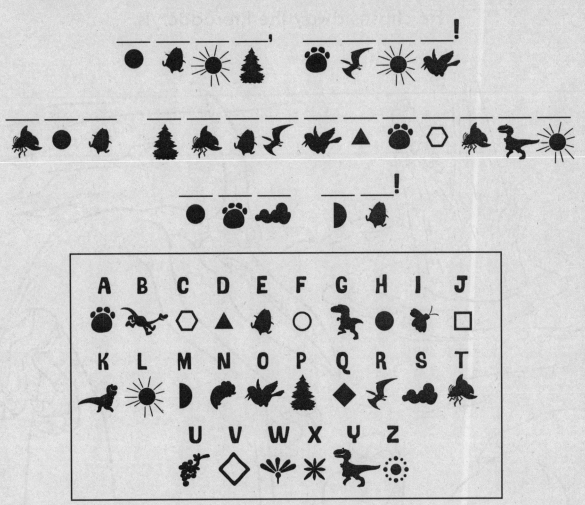

ANSWER: Help, Arlo! The Pterodactyl has me!

ArLo courageously races to save **Spot.**
He chases away the Pterodactyls.

Count the number of footprints.

ANSWER: 42.

Bug battle! With a friend, take turns drawing a line to connect two dots. If the line you draw completes a box, give yourself one point. When no more boxes can be made, the player with more points wins.

Play again! With a friend, take turns drawing a line to connect two dots. If the line you draw completes a box, give yourself one point. When no more boxes can be made, the player with more points wins.

Look at the two pictures.
Can you find three differences in the bottom picture?

To reveal the message, cross out all the *T*s and write the remaining letters in order on the line.

TTTHTETTATTTDTITNG THOTTMTETTT

_____ _____!

ANSWER: Heading home!

To reveal the message, start at the arrow and, going clockwise around the circle, write every other letter on the line.

Spot sees

_____   _____ .

Put the words in the correct boxes to complete the puzzle.

CLAWS • FEET • HANDS • HEADS • LEGS • TAILS • HORNS

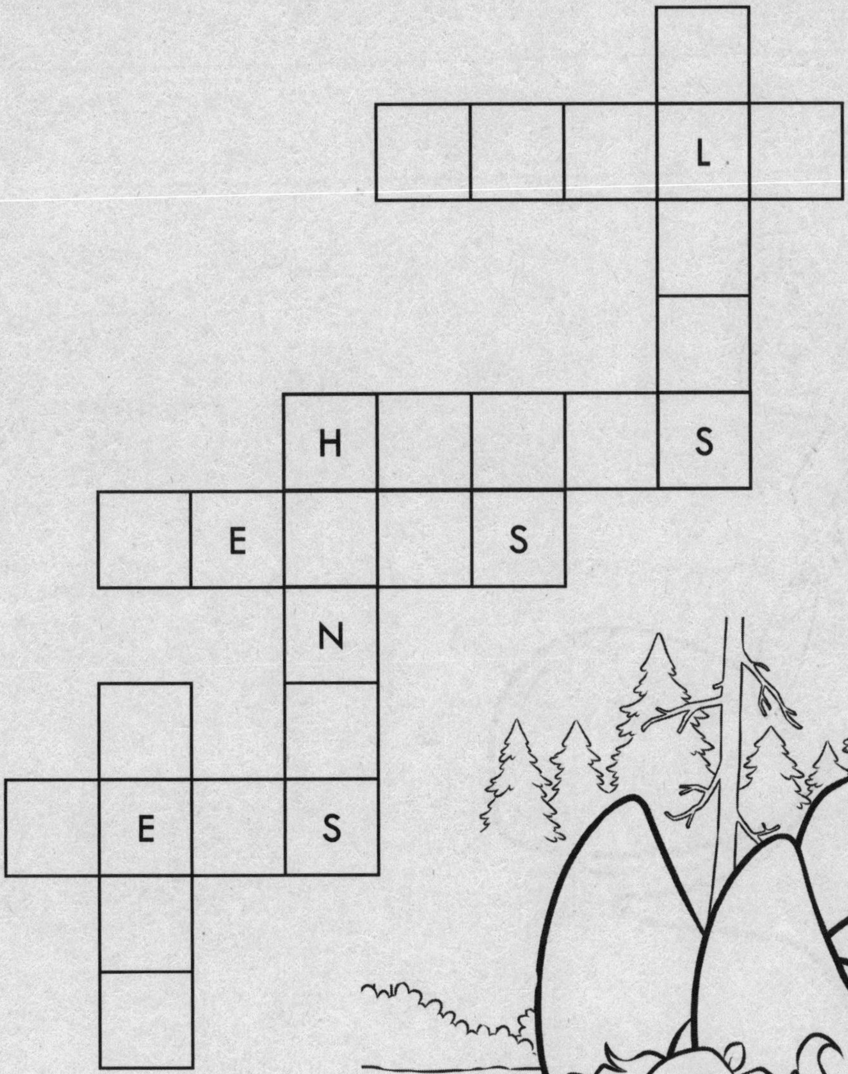

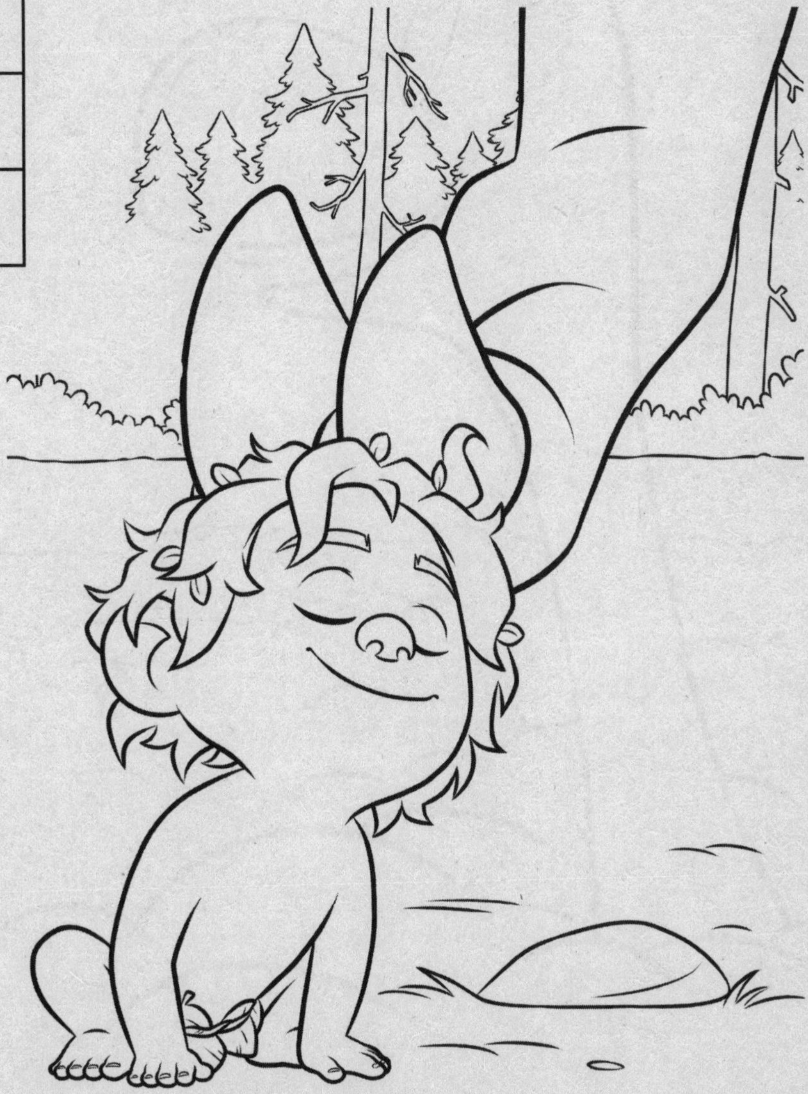

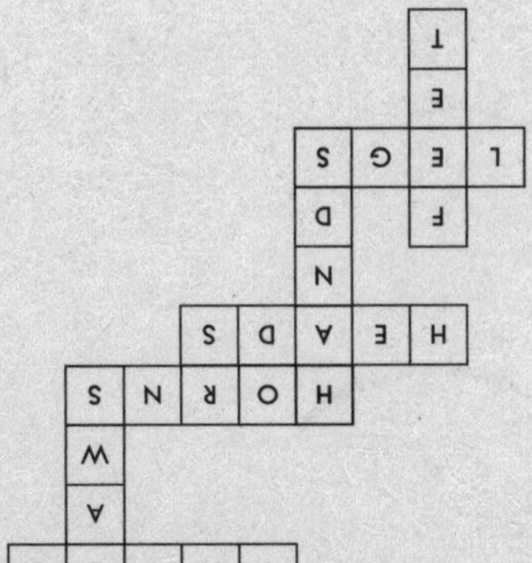

Arlo and **Spot** see Clawtooth Mountain.
Can you draw it?

The Pterodactyls are coming. Solve the maze to get away.

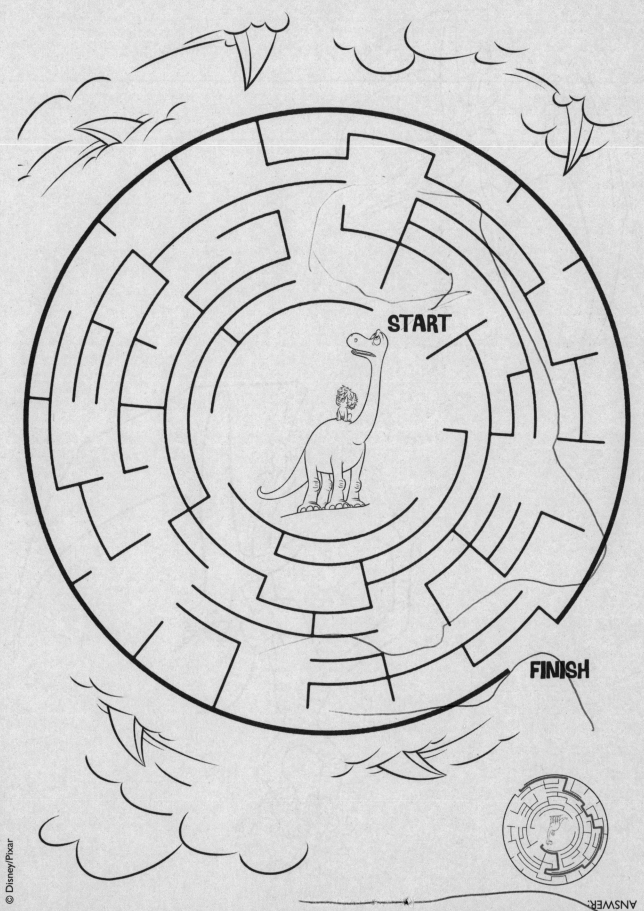

START

FINISH

ANSWER:

Add what is missing in the bottom picture.

Circle three things that are different in the bottom picture.

ANSWER: Arlo's pupils are white, there is a footprint missing on the wall, and one of Arlo's nostrils is missing.

Solve the maze in **Arlo's** mark.

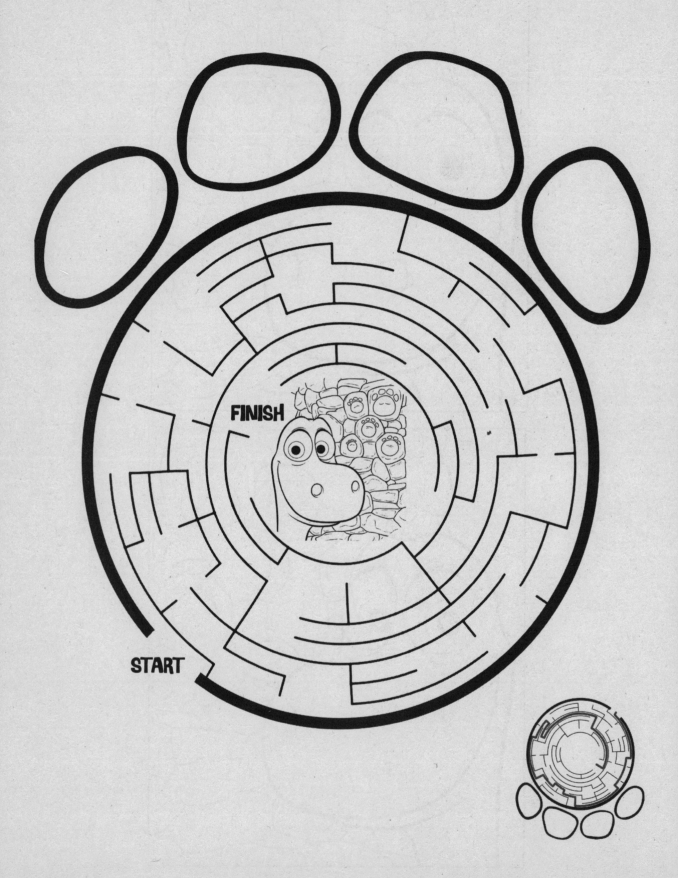

START

FINISH

Who is missing from this picture?
Can you add the missing dinosaur?

ANSWER: Arlo.

Look at the two pictures.
Find three differences in the bottom picture.

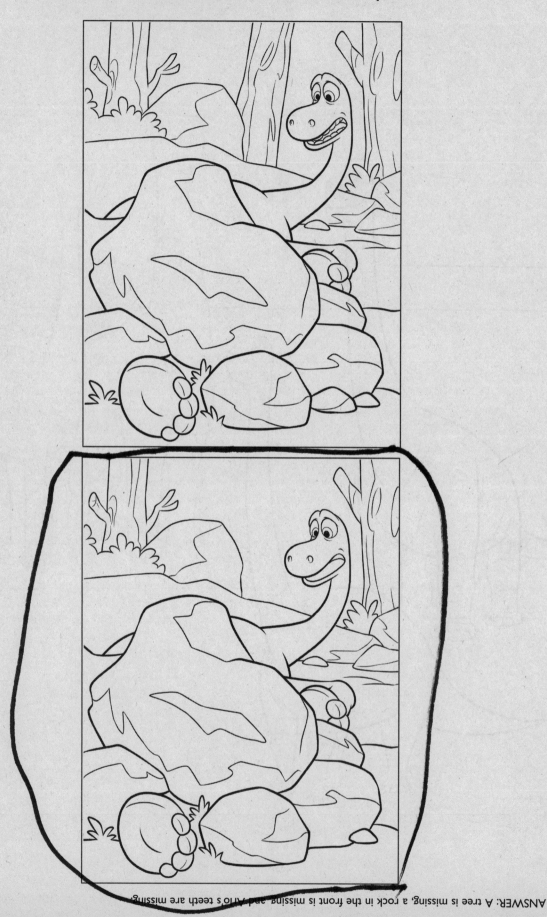

Connect the dots.

Use the key to color the picture.

1 = Green   2 = Brown   3 = Red   4 = Tan

Draw a creature for this beast to battle.

Help **Spot** find five things that begin with the letter S.
Look around the room you are in and write down five things
that start with S as quickly as possible.

_____

_____

_____

_____

_____

Draw horns and a neck frill on **Forrest Woodbush.**

It's a Raptor roundup! With a friend, take turns drawing a line to connect two dots. If the line you draw completes a box, give yourself one point. When no more boxes can be made, the player with more points wins.

Play again! With a friend, take turns drawing a line to connect two dots. If the line you draw completes a box, give yourself one point. When no more boxes can be made, the player with more points wins.

What is this bird's name? Use the code to find out.

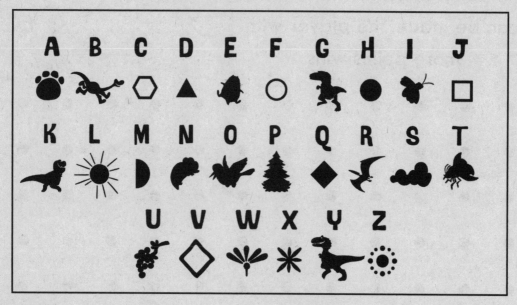

Having a friend is great! List your three favorite things about your best friend.

_____

_____

_____

Match the numbered piece of the picture with the identical scrambled piece from the picture below it. Write the correct number under each scrambled piece. For added fun, have an adult help you cut out the scrambled pieces. Then put them together in the correct order, just like a puzzle!

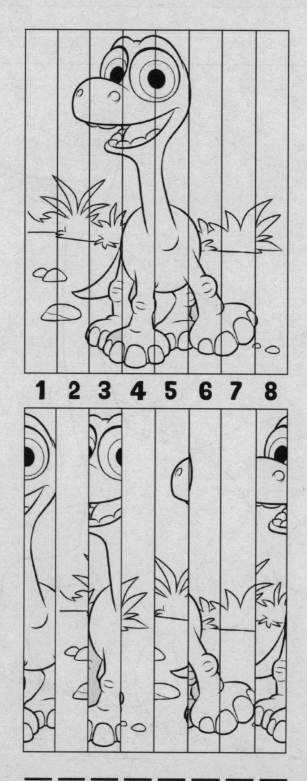

1 2 3 4 5 6 7 8

Circle the shadow that matches the picture.

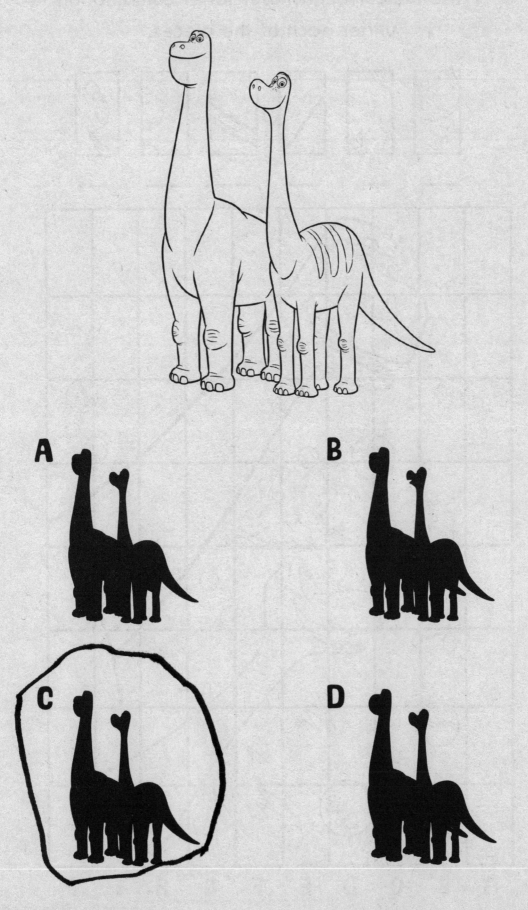

ANSWER: C.

Find each of the pieces in the picture grid.
Write the correct number-letter combination
under each of the pieces.

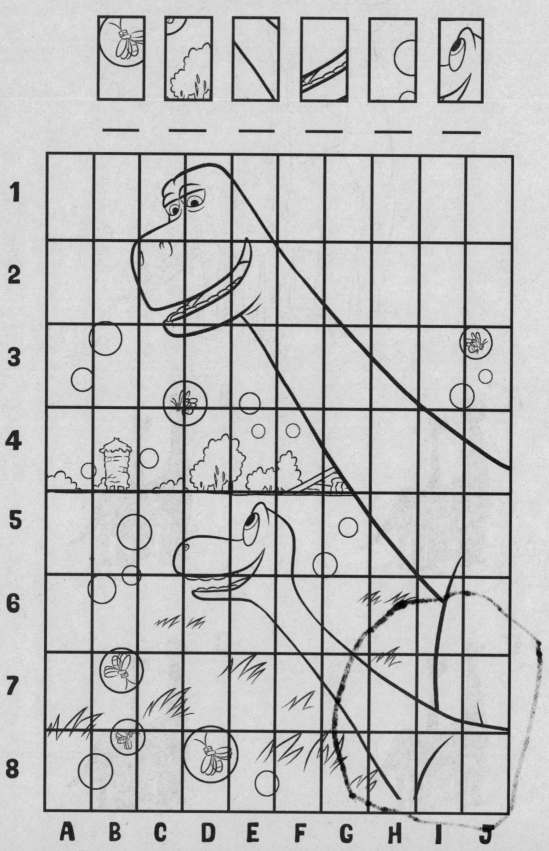

___   ___   ___   ___   ___   ___

A   B   C   D   E   F   G   H   I   J

Something has startled Arlo.
Connect the dots to find out what it is!

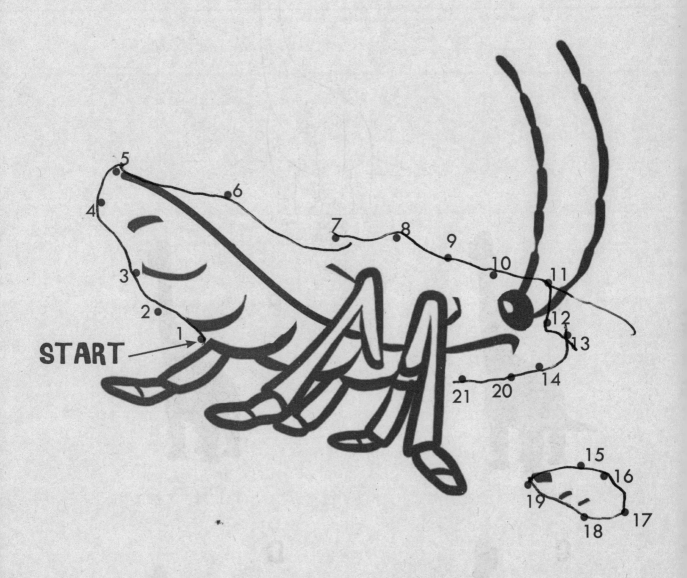

START

Look at the picture of Poppa.
Circle the shadow that matches the picture exactly.

A

B

C

D

How many 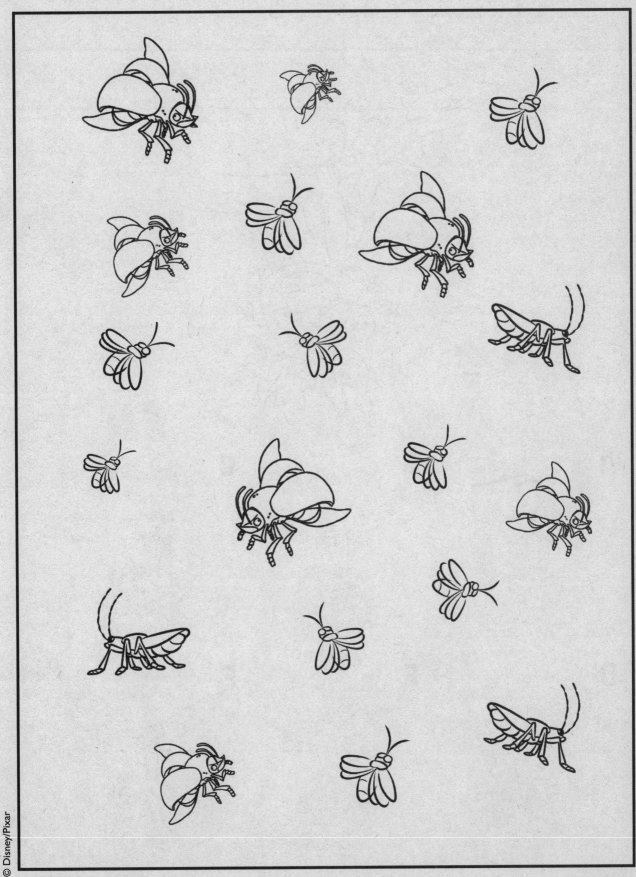 do you count?

Circle the two smaller pictures that are exactly the same as the larger one.

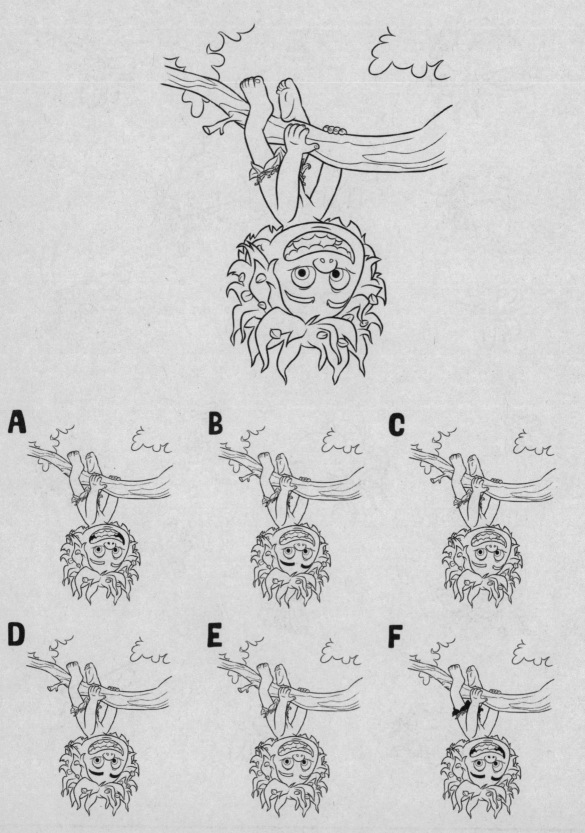

A

B

C

D

E

F

Help Arlo get to shore! Which line leads Arlo to Spot?

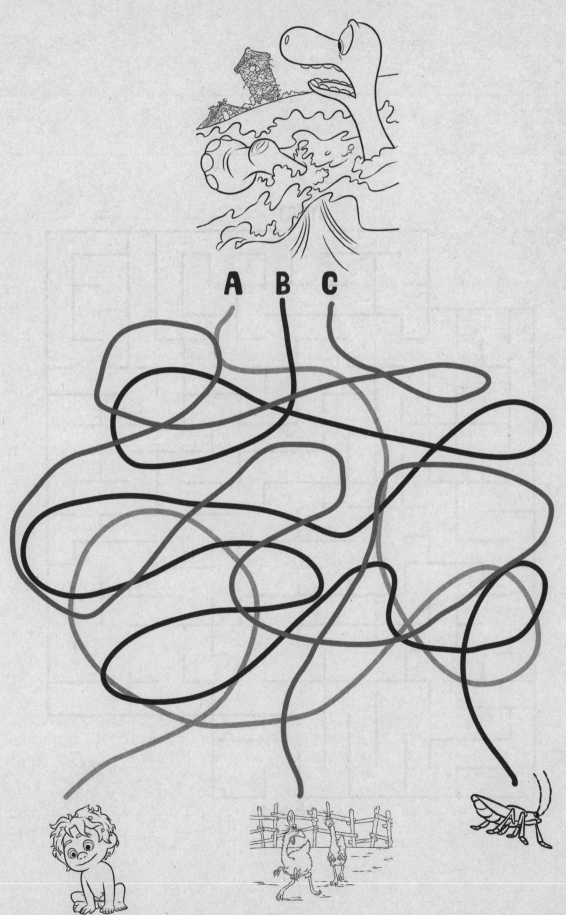

A   B   C

Help Arlo follow the river to his home.

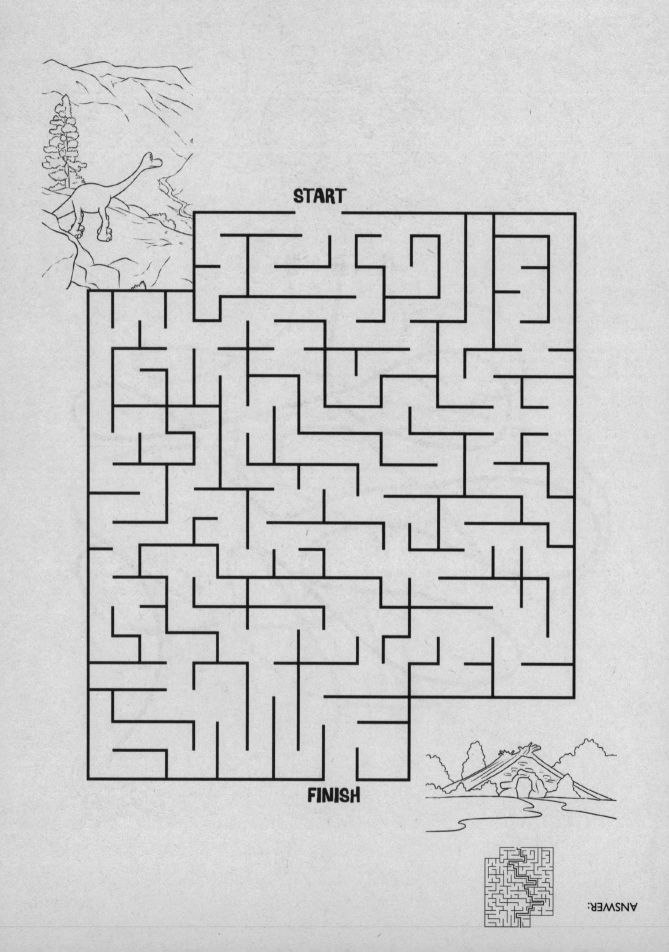

START

FINISH

Use the color key to color the picture.

1 = Brown   **2** = Black   **3** = Green   **4** = Blue

How many times can you find SPOT in the grid?
Look up, down, backward, forward, and diagonally.

```
S  O  P  S  P  S  T
P  P  T  P  S  P  O
O  S  T  O  P  S  T
S  P  O  T  O  P  S
P  S  S  O  T  P  O
O  P  O  P  O  T  T
T  O  P  S  P  T  S
T  S  P  O  S  S  P
```

ANSWER: 8.

Forrest's bird, Debbie, is very upset. He can hear her, but he is not sure where she is. Look at the picture below. Then find and circle Debbie.

ANSWER:

Draw a grid like the one here on a separate sheet of paper. To draw your own picture of Ramsey, copy the pictures on each square at a time, onto your blank grid.

Help the T. rexes find the rustling Raptors!
Follow the lines to see which one leads to the Raptors.

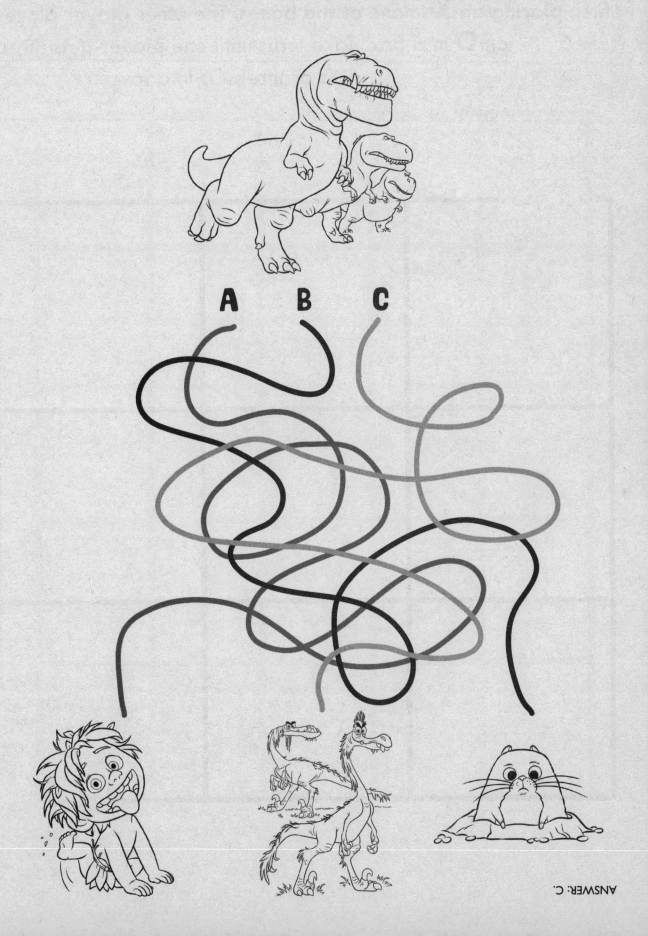

A B C

ANSWER: C.

Play a game of tic-tac-toe with a friend. Flip a coin to see who is **Arlo** and who is **Butch**. The player who is **Arlo** can go first, placing an **X** in one of the boxes. The other player places an **O** in a box. Take turns until one player gets three Xs or three Os in a row.

Arlo can't wait to get home! Finish the crossword puzzle to find out all the things **Arlo** will see at his family farm.

DOWN

1. Who is Poppa's only daughter?
2. Who is Arlo's mother?

ACROSS

3. Who is Arlo's brother?
4. What will Arlo find at the homestead?

ANSWER: 1. Libby, 2. Momma, 3. Buck, and 4. family.

ArLo is trying to rescue **Spot**.
Circle the nine differences in the bottom picture.

ANSWER:

Arlo shows **Spot** what his family looks like using twigs.
Draw your own family by creating twig figures.

To find out the names of the creatures,
put the letters in the correct order.

SOTPAAURSUA

_ _ _ _ _ _ _ _ _ _ _

DTPREOALYCT

_ _ _ _ _ _ _ _ _ _ _

XRTE

_ _ . _ _ _

RPTAOR

_ _ _ _ _ _

Spot and **Arlo** have too many berries for supper.
How many berries do you count?
(Remember to count the ones in Arlo's mouth.)

Which tracks belong to which characters?
Draw a line between each set of
tracks and the character they belong to.

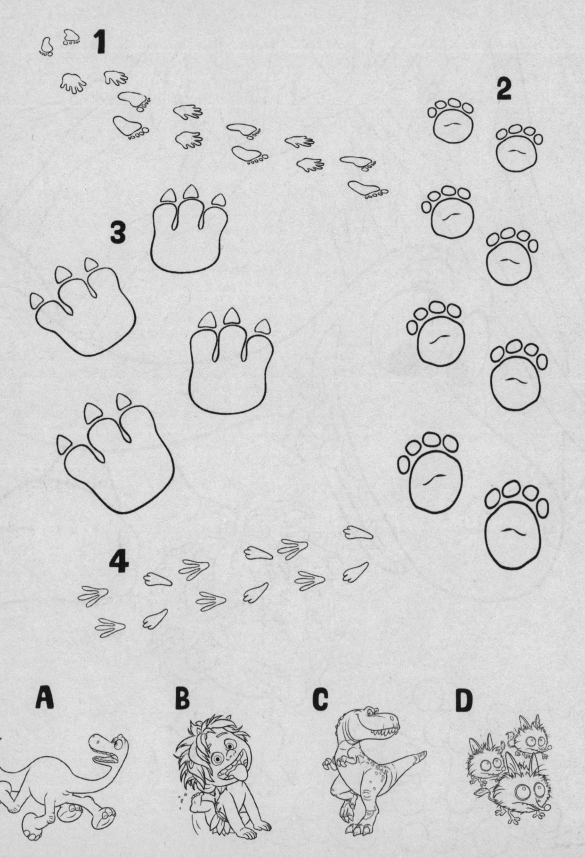

1

2

3

4

A **B** **C** **D**

What are the names of Arlo's brother and sister?

To find out, start with the letter *B* and, going clockwise around the circle twice, write every other letter in the blanks.

_ _ _ _   _ _ _   _ _ _ _ _

START

Decode the names below to find out whose mark is whose.

1. _ _ _ _ _

2. _ _ _ _ _

3. _ _ _ _ _ _

4. _ _ _ _

Find only the paths that lead to the letters in the word MOMMA.

© Disney/Pixar